Half for You and Half for Me

Half for You and Half for Me

BEST-LOVED NURSERY RHYMES
and the STORIES BEHIND THEM

KATHERINE GOVIER

illustrated by SARAH CLEMENT

whitecap

EDITED BY: Jenny Govier
DESIGNED BY: Andrew Bagatella
PROOFREAD BY: Theresa Best and Naomi Pauls

Printed in Canada

"Now if one day upon the street" and "Where 'ere you are this much I know," page 152, from R. and L. Page, *Wisdom from Nonsense Land*, Victoria, BC: Porcepic Books, 1991. Reprinted with permission of the estate of P.K Page. "Orders," page 158, from A.M. Klein, *Complete Poems: Part One*, edited by Zailig Pollock, Toronto: University of Toronto Press, 1990. Reprinted with permission of the publisher. "There is no Frigate like a Book," page 171, from *The Poems of Emily Dickinson: Variorum Edition*, edited by Ralph W. Franklin, Cambridge, MA: The Belknap Press of Harvard University Press, Copyright 1951, 1955, 1979, 1983, 1998 by the President and Fellows of Harvard College. "Night Thanks," page 178, from Dennis Lee, *So Cool*, Toronto: Key Porter Books, 2004. Reprinted with permission of the author.

Historical illustrations appear with the kind permission of the Osborne Collection of Early Children's Books in the Toronto Public Library.

Library and Archives Canada Cataloguing in Publication

Govier, Katherine, 1948-, author
  Half for you and half for me : best-loved nursery rhymes and the stories behind them / Katherine Govier ; illustrated by Sarah Clement.
Includes index.
ISBN 978-1-77050-212-3 (bound)
  1. Nursery rhymes. 2. Nursery rhymes--History and criticism.
I. Clement, Sarah, 1986-, illustrator II. Title.
PZ8.3.G685 2014   398.8
C2013-908278-6

The publisher acknowledges the financial support of the Canada Council for the Arts, the British Columbia Arts Council and the Government of Canada through the Canada Book Fund (CBF). Whitecap Books also acknowledges the financial support of the Province of British Columbia through the Book Publishing Tax Credit.

14 15 16 17 18   5 4 3 2 1

Canada Council   Conseil des Arts
for the Arts   du Canada

BRITISH COLUMBIA
ARTS COUNCIL
Supported by the Province of British Columbia

For my mother,

Doris Govier,

with love and gratitude

CONTENTS

ACKNOWLEDGMENTS

You cannot write about nursery rhymes without owing a huge debt, as I do, to Peter and Iona Opie, authors of *The Oxford Dictionary of Nursery Rhymes*. I wish to acknowledge their fascinating and extensive publications on nursery rhymes and the stories behind them as both inspiration and a source of information. My other main sources have been *Gammer Gurton's Garland* by Joseph Ritson and *The Annotated Mother Goose* by Cecil and William Baring-Gould. I've had a chance to look at these and some early Canadian sources, as well as many historical illustrations, in the Osborne Collection of Early Children's Books in the Toronto Public Library. I am grateful to Senior Department Head Leslie McGrath for her expertise and generosity with the collection.

THANK YOU TOO, TO MOTHER GOOSE, WHOEVER SHE WAS

Did she even exist? While Americans claim her, the French seem to have it in the bag. A French legend portrays Goose-Footed Bertha at her spinning wheel surrounded by a cluster of children listening to her stories. In France in 1697, Charles Perrault published *Tales of My Mother Goose*—children's stories, not rhymes. The name was first published in English in a 1729 translation of Perrault's book.

However, some Americans think Mother Goose is their own. A certain Elizabeth Forst Goose—or Vergoose—of Boston married Isaac Goose and managed to raise sixteen children. Her daughter married a Boston printer who claimed to have published his mother-in-law's stories as *Songs for the Nursery or Mother Goose's Melodies* ten years before Perrault. But no copy has ever been found. Her grave, in the Granary Burying Ground in Boston, even has a plaque. But it seems that particular Mother Goose is a pretender.

The author and her mother, Doris. Photo by George Govier.

READING WITH MUM

Ninety-five years ago, when my mother was born, her parents bought a beautiful book: *The Jessie Willcox Smith Mother Goose*. They read it to her while she sat on their knees. When she was old enough for crayons and scissors, she expressed her affection all over the pages. She kept it until she grew up and became a mother. I have a picture of Mum reading to me; I am about two, and I am entranced. I remember how she laughed. I loved the fact that words on a page could make her laugh.

Thirty years passed and I had two children of my own. When we visited their grandparents, the *Mother Goose* came out, and we read together. Now my kids are grown up. Soon I may have grandchildren. And my beautiful young mother has become one of those bent old women we saw in the pictures.

This year she gave me her vintage *Mother Goose*. Antiquarians say the Jessie Willcox Smith collection is the best ever published, with its beautiful colour plates and lovely thick paper. A good-condition copy sells for $750. But ours is falling apart, its spine like shredded wheat, its pages floating, cut up and crayoned upon.

Mum and I leaf through it (carefully). Her vision is clouded with macular degeneration. Possibly the greatest reader in the world, she now has trouble making out letters. She can't remember what I told her before lunch. But she does remember

Hark, hark, the dogs do bark,
The beggars are coming to town.
Some in rags and some in jags
And one in a velvet gown.

We wonder what it means. I tell Mum I've read that in Elizabethan times, roaming beggars threatened people in lonely villages. But "beggars" may also refer to the Dutch, who invaded England in 1688, overthrowing King James II; the one in velvet might be King William of Orange himself. "Imagine that!" I tell Mum . . . We turn the page. "Mary, Mary, quite contrary . . ." She recites the rest of that one too.

Why do ancient nursery rhymes stick fast in our minds when what we did yesterday slides away? Is it because of the scary visions they conjure—gangs of motley beggars setting off the dogs, kittens down wells, children brained with clubs? Because we heard them when we were so young? Because they are mysterious?

Do we love the rhymes just for themselves, the way they bounce and repeat? Their sounds are as rich as their wisdom is questionable. They are charming in their nonsense—and striking in their logic.

There was an old woman
Lived under a hill
And if she's not gone,
She lives there still.

Is part of the secret to the endurance of nursery rhymes their immediacy? Each one seems to be a moment preserved in amber, a tiny incident, real and particular—a girl frightened by a spider, a boy falling asleep when he's supposed to be watching sheep.

I'm not sure.

I only know that Mum gave me more than this tattered treasure. She gave me my love of words. My awe at the power of a few lines on a page. Often when I'm writing, a Humpty Dumpty or a Wee Willie Winkie elbows his way into the front of my shop window of phrases, displaying his cadences and dire consequences. "Beat them all soundly and put them to bed." "Your house is on fire and your children all gone!" Countless other writers have given nursery rhyme characters moments in novels and popular songs. The farmer's wife with her carving knife and her fellows appear throughout art, advertising and film.

The violent ends these characters meet thrilled me, once. Nothing better than hearing about dread consequences from the security of my mother's lap! The world was out there and it was dangerous. But it's been a long time since I tucked myself into Mum's side and stared at the pages, hoping to learn to read by osmosis. Now as much as nursery rhymes delight me, they make me curious. What real incidents lie behind the stories? Why are they full of mishaps and murder? Yes, children's lives were more violent three or four hundred years ago. But there are other reasons.

The oldest rhymes were not intended for the nursery. They were not for children. They were for adults, repeated by the irreverent and mostly powerless population to mark events, satirize the powerful or pass judgment. Quite often they can be read as code.

Many scholars have opined on their meanings. "In their seeming lightness are portrayed the tragedies of kings and queens, the corruptions of opposing political parties, and stories of fanatical religious strife," said Katherine E. Thomas of Boston,

quoted by Cecil and William Baring-Gould in *The Annotated Mother Goose*. One professor did the math, to discover that half the rhymes in an average collection "harbour unsavoury elements." He counted "8 allusions to murder, 2 cases of choking to death, 1 case of death by devouring, 1 case of cutting a human being in half, 1 case of decapitation, 1 case of death by squeezing," and 16 further allusions to misery and sorrow. We can hold with psychologist Bruno Bettelheim, who says in *The Uses of Enchantment* (1976) that the demons in fairy tales symbolize a child's destructive urges and enable him to overcome them. Or we can just conclude that violent deeds and evildoers are there because they are part of life. I prefer the latter. "The nursery rhyme is the novel and light reading of the infant scholar," says James Orchard Halliwell in *The Nursery Rhymes of England*, published in 1886.

But like many a novel the rhymes seem to have a double purpose, both to entertain and to teach. When first published, Mother Goose's nursery rhymes appeared with a moral—never what you imagine and often quite funny. Over centuries the more ghoulish ones were cleaned up or misremembered or updated. In the older rhymes we discover lost bits of our language—curses and jokes and street vendors' cries. We glimpse village life, its characters, its gossip and its nightmare

scenes—marching armies and women in the stocks. There's history to be learned, but of the best kind, born in the gritty and petty everyday.

Children aren't the only ones who love rhythm, wordplay and pratfalls. I hope you read nursery rhymes as we did in our family: together. This collection aims to amuse the adult as well as the toddler.

My mother made up her own rhyme last summer as we were reading over the manuscript for this book on holiday in the Rockies. Future decoders may find in it a critique of the accessibility features in the Jasper Park Lodge. Then again it may mean something much more ancient.

As well as the old, I've included some contemporary and lesser-known rhymes with the hope of nudging them into the canon. My family has English, Irish, French and American roots and these were the rhymes we knew. What I haven't done is reflect the many cultures alive in Canada today. Friends from other parts of the globe say that if you grow up with two languages at home you hear nursery rhymes in each. It seems these little verses don't translate easily. It would be fun to try—but that's another book.

I hear contradictory answers to the question "Are they still in use?" Are girls skipping to "On a mountain stands a lady"? I hope so. You tell me!

irls and boys, come out to play
The moon doth shine as bright
        as day.
Leave your supper and leave your sleep
And come with your playfellows into
        the street.
Come with a whoop, come with a call
And come with a good will or come not
        at all.
Up the ladder and down the wall,
A halfpenny loaf will serve us all.
You find milk and I'll find flour
And we'll have a pudding in half an hour.
Salt, vinegar, mustard, pepper!

One of the oldest nursery rhymes in existence, this reflects a time when children worked in the daytime, only going out to play at night when work was done. It likely dates from the 1600s and was sung in the south of France by girls who did ring dances in public squares. When the clocks struck ten they turned themselves in, singing

Ten hours said! Maids to bed.

The song appeared in England a century later, eventually crossed the Atlantic and was heard in nineteenth-century American streets. In the late 1950s, in the playground of Windsor Park School in Edmonton, Alberta, we sang the last line while skipping. On the word "pepper!" we turned the rope as fast as possible.

The original moral, according to my *Mother Goose,* is: "All work and no play makes Jack a dull boy."

FIRST THINGS

Here we go round the mulberry bush,
The mulberry bush,
The mulberry bush.
Here we go round the mulberry bush
So early in the morning.

This rhyme has been co-opted by a prison. There was a mulberry tree in the yard of Her Majesty's Prison at Wakefield, Yorkshire, England. The female prisoners exercised around it. A recent prison governor, R.S. Duncan, has written a book, *Here We Go Round the Mulberry Bush: The House of Correction 1595/HM Prison Wakefield 1995,* giving the details. But experts dispute the prison's claim.

Wakefield has housed many of Britain's most famous and dangerous prisoners. No women are held there now. It is a supermax institution; as such it is highly contentious, as many believe these institutions contravene the inmates' human rights.

More mundanely, in many homes the verse goes on to describe morning activities or weekly chores:

This is the way we wash the clothes
Wash the clothes
Wash the clothes.
This is the way we wash the clothes
So early Monday morning.

One, two, buckle my shoe
Three, four, shut the door
Five, six, pick up sticks
Seven, eight, lay them straight
Nine, ten, a big, fat hen
Eleven, twelve, dig and delve
Thirteen, fourteen, maids a-courting
Fifteen, sixteen, maids in the kitchen
Seventeen, eighteen, maids a-waiting
Nineteen, twenty, my plate's empty.

Hickory, dickory, dock
The mouse ran up the clock
The clock struck one
The mouse ran down
Hickory, dickory, dock.

The words "hickory," "dickory" and "dock" mean eight,
nine and ten in an ancient counting system used by
shepherds in parts of England near the Scottish border. In
Cumbria and Westmorland, forms of the *yan, tan, tethera*
system of numbers survived until the nineteenth century
as a way for shepherds to perform head counts on their
flocks. The words derive from the Celtic language. Children
used the counting system to determine who started first
in games. In my *Mother Goose* this rhyme appeared with
the moral "Time stays [stops] for no man." It's a sober one,
which no two-year-old understands. But for me, reading
with my aged mother, it is sharp and painful.

wist me, and turn me, and show me
the elf;
I looked in the water, and saw [myself].

This is from *The Brownies and Other Tales,* by Juliana Horatia
Ewing. She lived in New Brunswick for four years and so we
count her as Canadian.

What is a Brownie? Before it was a junior Girl Guide,
it was "a useful little fellow, something like a little man." How
do you find one? Go to the north side of the lake when the
moon is shining and turn yourself round three times, saying
this charm. When the child looks in the water, he either says
his name, "Jimmie!" or "myself!"

GENTLE GAMES

Pat-a-cake, pat-a-cake, baker's man
Bake me a cake as fast as you can
Roll it, and prick it and mark it with B
Throw it in the oven for baby and me.

This hand game for babies dates as far back as the
seventeenth century. Originally there were two voices in
it, the baker's and that of his (or possibly her) man. The
person holding the baby pats the two little hands together
on "pat," rubs them together on "roll it," and on "prick it,"
the baby's forefinger on his right hand pokes the palm of his
left. On "throw it in the oven," both hands are thrown up.

ere is the church and here is
the steeple

Open the doors and here are the people.

Clasp hands together so that fingers are intertwined inside
and pointer fingers form a steeple. On the second line, open
the thumb "doors," then turn your hands palm-side up and
wiggle the "people" in their seats.

nky Dinky spider went up the
water spout

Down came the rain and washed the
spider out
Out came the sun and dried up all
the rain
And Inky Dinky spider went up the
spout again.

Another finger game: Adult fingers step their way up a small
arm, fall off with the rain, then try again.

ere sits the Lord Mayor
Here sit his two men
Here sits the cock
Here sits the hen
Here sit the little chickens
Here they run in.
Chinchopper, chinchopper,
    chinchopper chin!

This rhyme appears, with instructions, in *Young Canada's Nursery Rhymes,* published in 1888. The instructions describe the grownup touching the child, in succession, on forehead (Lord Mayor), eyes (two men), right cheek and left cheek (cock and hen), tip of nose (little chickens) and mouth (they run in), and then chucking the chin on "chinchopper."

ide a cock-horse to Banbury Cross
To see a fine lady upon a white horse.
Rings on her fingers and bells on her toes
And she shall have music wherever
she goes.

A cock-horse is a toy or wooden horse. When this rhyme is recited the horse can be a grownup's knee. Another meaning was the extra horse, or "coach" horse, that was added to a team to pull a coach up a hill. Bells were commonly worn on the long pointed toes of shoes in the fifteenth century, so the rhyme could be that old. Some accounts say that the "fine lady" was Queen Elizabeth I, others that she was Lady Godiva. In which case, aside from the rings and bells, she wore nothing.

his is the way the ladies ride
Trip trot trip.
This is the way the gentlemen ride
Jimmy Jimmy.
This is the way the farmers ride
Hobbledee hoy, hobbledee hoy.

This bouncing game begins at a sedate, lady-like pace, then becomes more aggressive but still civilized. When you get to the farmer, the baby is jiggling madly. Unaware of its commentary on class differences, I loved this rhyme for the chance to make funny noises— sometimes the farmers rode "gobbledee gook"; sometimes the ladies rode "shellack, shellack."

TO WORK

Little Bo-Peep
Has lost her sheep
And can't tell where to find them.
Leave them alone
And they'll come home
Wagging their tails behind them.

"It's not wagging but dragging," says Mum. "They were tired and worn out and a little bit ashamed." Of course she's right. That's all I ever knew, but there's more:

> Bo-Peep fell fast asleep
> And dreamt she heard them bleating.
> But when she awoke, she found it a joke
> For they were still a-fleeting.
>
> Then up she took her little crook
> Determined for to find them.
> She found them indeed, but it made her heart bleed
> For they'd left their tails behind them.
>
> It happened one day, as Bo-Peep did stray
> Into a meadow hard by
> There she espied their tails side by side
> All hung on a tree to dry.
>
> She heaved a sigh and wiped her eye
> And over the hillocks went rambling
> And tried what she could, as a shepherdess should,
> To tack each again to its lambkin.

"Bo-peep" meant "peek-a-boo." In medieval times if you were convicted of a crime you might have to "play bo pepe throwe a pillery"—be put in the pillory, or stocks, with your head and arms peeping out. How the shepherdess got involved is anyone's guess.

Little Boy Blue

Come blow your horn
The sheep's in the meadow,
The cow's in the corn.
Where is that boy
Who looks after the sheep?
Under the haystack
Fast asleep.
Will you wake him?
Oh no, not I,
For if I do
He will surely cry.

A touching rhyme when you think the boy had a job 'though he was so young he would cry if chided. L. Frank Baum (author of *The Wonderful Wizard of Oz*) wrote a story portraying Little Boy Blue as a victim of child labour.

Jack and Jill went up the hill
To fetch a pail of water.
Jack fell down and broke his crown
And Jill came tumbling after.

Up Jack got, and home did trot
As fast as he could caper
To old Dame Dob, who patched his nob
With vinegar and brown paper.

Then Jill came in, and she did grin
To see Jack's paper plaster;
Her mother whipt her across her knee
For laughing at Jack's disaster.

There are many wild assertions about the origins of this well-known rhyme. Because the pair goes uphill to get water, which is usually found at the bottom of hills, the Norse moon god is suspected of playing a part. But another view is that the first verse refers to King Charles I, who ordered the size of a "jack"—a half pint—to be reduced so that he could get his tax, his "crown." Still, a village in Somerset, England, claims that the accident happened right there. Vinegar and brown paper was a home remedy.

Bye, Baby Bunting,
Daddy's gone a-hunting,
Gone to get a rabbit skin
To wrap the Baby Bunting in.

When this appeared in *Gammer Gurton's Garland* in 1810, "bunting" was a pet name meaning plump. I thought it was a baby wrap, but apparently not. A longer version appeared twenty years later:

> Bye, Baby Bunting,
> Daddy's gone a-hunting
> Mother's gone a-milking
> Sister's gone a-silking
> Brother's gone to buy a skin
> To wrap the Baby Bunting in.

Sister's gone a-silking? Women worked in the silk industry in England as early as the fourteenth century. Huguenots, Protestants who fled religious persecution in France, swelled their numbers.

This little piggy went to market
This little piggy stayed home
This little piggy had roast beef
This little piggy had none
And this little piggy went wee wee wee
        all the way home.

Delicious trepidation, knowing that on the last line the
grownup's fingers would march up my leg and into my armpit,
where they would dig in and tickle me so hard I'd scream. This
rhyme has been popular for more than a century. You have to
wonder what vegetarian parents are going to do with it.

urly locks, curly locks, wilt thou
    be mine?
Thou shall't not wash dishes, nor yet feed
    the swine,
But sit on a cushion and sew a fine seam
And feed upon strawberries, sugar
    and cream!

A wooing song that shows curly hair was something to be
desired and admired. Until recently. This constituted a vision
of marital bliss: to work sitting down, "sew a fine seam" and
eat lady-like sweets as a woman of leisure.

Half a pound of tuppenny rice
Half a pound of treacle.
That's the way the money goes
Pop goes the weasel.

A penny for a spool of thread
A penny for a needle.
That's the way the money goes
Pop goes the weasel.

In the seventeenth century, immigrants and the poor worked in London's textile industry in Spitalfields. This might be a work song, designed to keep pace with the looms. A spinner's weasel was shaped like a spoked wheel; it measured out yarn and gave a "pop" when the desired length was reached.

"Pop Goes the Weasel" was popular as a music-hall song in Victorian London, before being spun off into numerous verses and variations.

STREET CRIES

Before the days of supermarkets, you might have heard these when you went out shopping.

If I'd as much money as I could spend
I never would cry "Old chairs to mend,"
Old chairs to mend, old chairs to mend,
I never would cry "Old chairs to mend."
If I'd as much money as I could tell
I never would cry "Old clothes to sell,"
Old clothes to sell, old clothes to sell,
I never would cry "Old clothes to sell."

Hot cross buns! Hot cross buns!
One a penny, two a penny, hot
        cross buns.
If you have no daughters, give them to
        your sons.
One a penny, two a penny, hot cross buns!

At the beginning of Lent, sharing a hot cross bun with another is supposed to ensure friendship throughout the coming year, particularly if

Half for you and half for me
Between us two shall goodwill be.

abbit, rabbit, rabbit pie!
Come, my ladies, come and buy
Else your babies they will cry.

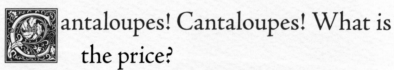

antaloupes! Cantaloupes! What is
   the price?
Eight for a dollar, and all very nice.

Piping hot!
Smoking hot!
What have I got you have not?
Hot grey peas, hot hot hot
Hot grey peas, hot!

The moral that appeared with this rhyme when it was first published? "There is more music in this song on a cold frosty night than ever the Sirens were possessed of who captivated Ulysses, and the effect sticks closer to the ribs."

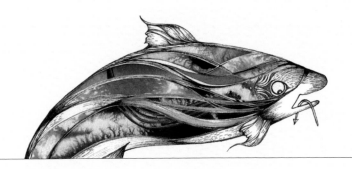

TO SCHOOL

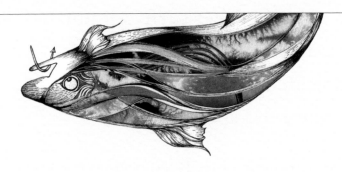

Mary had a little lamb
Whose fleece was white as snow
And everywhere that Mary went
The lamb was sure to go.

It followed her to school one day,
Which was against the rule.
It made the children laugh and play
To see a lamb at school.

And so the teacher turned it out
But still it lingered near
And waited patiently about
Till Mary did appear.

"Why does the lamb love Mary so?"
The eager children cry.
"Why, Mary loves the lamb, you know,"
The teacher did reply.

In Sterling, Massachusetts, a child named Mary Sawyer took her pet lamb to school. A visiting student minister wrote the first three verses; a statue of the lamb still stands in the town centre. Thomas Edison contributed to the fame of this rhyme by making it the first to be recorded on his phonograph, in 1877.

The illustration comes from the version of the rhyme illustrated by W.W. Denslow. Famed as the illustrator of *The Wonderful Wizard of Oz*, Denslow always added a seahorse to his signature.

A diller, a dollar, a ten o'clock scholar
What makes you come so soon?
You used to come at ten o'clock
But now you come at noon.

If I was you and you was me
(Which never, never, never could be
Because the grammar is bad, you see)
But, if I were you, and you were I,
When one got hurt, which one would cry?

Why are the authors and illustrators of children's rhymes so little known? This rhyme is taken from the first colour illustrated Canadian children's book, *Uncle Jim's Canadian Nursery Rhymes for Home and Kindergarten.* It was written by Dr. David Boyle, considered the father of Canadian archaeology, for his granddaughter Adele. The book was illustrated by Charles William Jefferys, "still regarded as the dean of Canadian historical draughtsmen."

The very rare book with its beautiful pictures lives in the Osborne Collection, along with a pamphlet entitled *Under Some Malignant Star,* chronicling the venture. The publisher's British printer went bankrupt and did not return the artwork. Twenty years later the art turned up in a London auction house and was sold for five pounds before its creator could get a bid in. The Canadian purchaser had the nerve to ask Jefferys to sign the plates. The illustrator declined—by then his signature was worth something. Eventually a well-wisher bought the illustrations and gave them to Jefferys.

apple pie

B bit it

C cut it

D dealt it

E eat it

F fought for it

G got it

H had it

I impede it

J joined it

K kept it

L longed for it

M mourned for it

N nodded at it

O opened it
P peeped in it
Q quartered it
R run at it
S stole it
T took it
U uplifted it
V viewed it
W wanted it
X, Y, Z and all wished for a piece in hand.

This rhyme originally appeared in a chapbook published in 1840 as *The Tragical Death of an Apple-Pie.* There have been many versions since then. In some versions a cautionary note to children about learning their alphabet appears after the title: "Which was cut to pieces and eaten by twenty-six persons, with whom all young folks ought to be well acquainted."

One, two, three, four, five
Once I caught a fish alive.
Six, seven, eight, nine, ten
Then I let it go again.
Why did you let it go?
Because it bit my finger so.
Which finger did it bite?
This little finger on my right.

Monday alone
Tuesday together
Wednesday we walk
When it's fine weather.
Thursday we kiss
Friday we cry
Saturday, hours
Seem almost to fly.
But of all the days in the week, we will call
Sunday, the rest day, the best day of all.

Of many nursery rhymes about the days of the week, this is my favourite. Shall we explain what rest days are? Mum points out that Methodists—my father's people—didn't work or read on Sunday. It was an enforced rest day. Some didn't even cook their dinner; they ate cold food, she says.

Monday's child is fair of face
Tuesday's child is full of grace
Wednesday's child is full of woe
Thursday's child has far to go.
Friday's child is loving and giving
Saturday's child works hard for a living
And the child who is born on the
                    Sabbath Day
Is bonny and blithe and good and gay.

Solomon Grundy
Born on a Monday
Christened on Tuesday
Married on Wednesday
Took ill on Thursday
Grew worse on Friday
Died on Saturday
Buried on Sunday.
That was the end
Of Solomon Grundy.

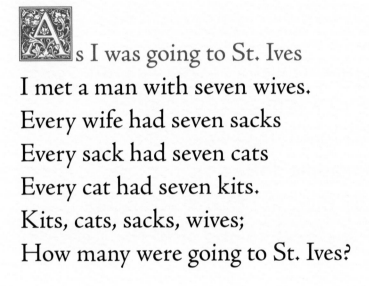

As I was going to St. Ives
I met a man with seven wives.
Every wife had seven sacks
Every sack had seven cats
Every cat had seven kits.
Kits, cats, sacks, wives;
How many were going to St. Ives?

(Answer: One: "I." The rest were going the other way.)

In marble walls as white as milk
Lined with a skin as soft as silk
Within a fountain crystal clear
A golden apple doth appear.
No doors there are to this stronghold
Yet thieves break in and steal the gold.

(Answer: An egg.)

Little Nancy Etticote
In a white petticoat
And a red nose;
The longer she stands,
The shorter she grows.

(Answer: A candle.)

OUTDOORS

It's raining, it's pouring
The old man is snoring
He bumped his head on the foot of
    the bed
And couldn't get up in the morning.

Doctor Foster went to Gloucester
In a shower of rain.
He stepped in a puddle
Right up to his middle
And never went there again.

This may describe the day, over seven hundred years ago, when King Edward I (1239–1307) went to Gloucester and rode his horse through what he thought was a shallow puddle. It wasn't. It was so deep that he and his horse got stuck in the mud and had to be pulled out with ropes. Edward was tall (they called him Longshanks) and temperamental, and generally considered to be a good, even a great king. Too bad he is remembered for this blooper.

How the rain pours
And the lightnings flash!
How the wind roars
And the thunders crash!
But my little baby is safe as can be
Cuddling here on mother's knee.

Another rhyme from the beautifully illustrated *Uncle Jim's Canadian Nursery Rhymes*. I too like to sit on someone's knee during thunderstorms.

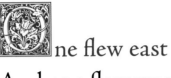ne flew east
And one flew west
And one flew over the cuckoo's nest.

This is one of the few Canadian nursery rhymes originating
in languages other than English that I've found in translation.
It began its life in modern low German and was translated and
published in *The Windmill Turning: Nursery Rhymes, Maxims,
and Other Expressions of Western Canadian Mennonites,* by
Victor Carl Friesen. Friesen explains it this way: When families
scatter, children can grow up to be irresponsible, escaping
family duties and even going so far as to act like the cuckoo,
which lays its eggs in other birds' nests. A longer rhyme
that also seems to have German roots, and was published in
England and popular in the United States, included these lines:

> Wire briar limber lock
> Three geese in a flock
> One flew east
> One flew west
> One flew over the cuckoo's nest.

The north wind doth blow and we
     shall have snow
And what will poor robin do then,
     poor thing?
He'll sit in a barn and keep himself warm
And hide his head under his wing,
     poor thing.

We did this verse at school, with actions. You try to hide your head under your arm. Other verses list small animals: the dormouse, for instance. And daisies. They were all to be pitied when winter comes. It seems like a poor attitude if you live in a northerly place.

Red sky in the morning,
Sailor take warning.
Red sky at night,
Sailor's delight.

Sailors and shepherds both take careful note of the weather. The saying is very old and likely to have been passed by word of mouth by shepherds before it was eventually written down by sailors.

If all the seas were one sea
What a great sea that would be!
If all the trees were one tree
What a great tree that would be!
If all the axes were one axe
What a great axe that would be!
If all the men were one man
What a great man he would be!
And if the great man took the great axe
And cut down the great tree
And let it fall into the great sea
What a great splash-splash that would be!

When zero comes and ground is hard
We take the hose and flood the yard.
I like the garden, but I think
I like it better as a rink.

By Robert Kay Gordon, this comes from *A Canadian Child's ABC*. It was published in 1931 with charming woodcuts by Thoreau MacDonald, son of Group of Seven member J.E.H. MacDonald. He was colour-blind so always worked in black and white.

Dad flooded our backyard. We skated there for hours, so close to the kitchen we could be waved in just as supper came onto the table.

CURIOUS CHARACTERS

Humpty Dumpty sat on a wall
Humpty Dumpty had a great fall.
All the King's horses and all the King's men
Could not put Humpty together again.

We imagine Humpty Dumpty as an egg, probably because his reassembly is hopeless. In other languages he is a drunk, or a dumpy person—*Boule Boule* in French and *Humpelken Pumpelken* in German.

Likely he was not a person at all, but a cannon set on a wall around the castle town of Colchester by royalists to protect it during a siege. When the wall collapsed and the cannon fell down, the royalists—"all the King's men"— could not put it back up. Carl Bernstein and Bob Woodward amended the phrase to title their book *All the President's Men,* about the Watergate scandal. Might does not always prevail. Something delicate may be broken that no power can patch up.

here was a crooked man
Who walked a crooked mile.
He found a crooked sixpence
Against a crooked stile.
He bought a crooked cat,
Which caught a crooked mouse,
And they all lived together
In a little crooked house.

There was an old woman who lived
in a shoe
She had so many children, she didn't
know what to do.
She gave them some porridge without
any bread
Then borrowed a beetle, and knocked 'em
on the head.
Then out went the old woman to bespeak
'em a coffin
And when she came back, she found 'em
all a loeffing.

Who are the villains here? The old woman who knocks
her children out and takes them for dead? Or the children
who "loeff" at her? That last word leads experts to date
this from Shakespeare's time. The shoe-dweller may be
England's King George II, who was mocked as an old woman
because his wife bossed him around and he couldn't control
his parliamentarians. But a more fertile line of approach
is to see her as a rattled mother. Why would she live in
a shoe? With all those children any space would seem
tight—as we would say, the size of a shoebox. Shoes were
symbolically connected with fertility; in certain parts of
England women who wanted to conceive would wear the
shoes of another who had just given birth. The Opies say
that the shoe was symbolic of "what is personal to a woman
until marriage." That's why we cast old shoes after the
bride when she goes off on her honeymoon.

Another old woman . . .

There was an old woman tossed up
   in a basket
Ninety times as high as the moon
And where she was going I couldn't but
   ask it
For in her hand she carried a broom.

Old woman, old woman, old woman,
   quoth I,
O whither, O whither, O whither so high?
To sweep the cobwebs off the sky.
Shall I go with you?
Aye, by and by.

If you wonder why there are so many old women in
nursery rhymes, consider that there were many in the
English population, too. As far back as 1750 it was noticed
that women outlived men, and anyone was "old" at forty.

There was an old woman
Lived under a hill
And if she's not gone,
She lives there still.

This was my introduction to elementary logic. It is known as
a self-evident proposition. But it wasn't always an old woman
sitting on that hill. In one iteration the rhyme ran

Pillycock, pillycock, sate on a hill
If he's not gone, he sits there still.

"Pillycock" is slang for phallus. Shakespeare lets Edgar repeat
the rhyme in *King Lear* when he is pretending to be mad:
"Pillicock sat on Pillicock Hill; alow, alow, loo, loo."

Ladybird, ladybird,
Fly away home.
Your house is on fire
And your children all gone.
All except one
And that's little Ann
And she has crept under
The warming pan.

This ancient rhyme can be found in similar form in France, Germany, Switzerland, Denmark, Russia and Sweden, even down to the detail of the name "Ann" for the child who escapes. The ladybird, or ladybug as we say in North America, was thought to be sacred. Its name comes from the Christian "Our Lady's Bird." In Hindu it is *Indragopa.* Some sources claim that the beetle's resemblance to an Egyptian scarab associates the rhyme with Isis. Others see evidence of worship of the Norse goddess Freya. When we found one, my friends and I would put the ladybug on the back of our hand or the end of our index finger and blow to make it fly away.

Peter, Peter, pumpkin eater,
Had a wife but couldn't keep her.
Put her in a pumpkin shell
And there he kept her very well.

Peter, Peter, pumpkin eater,
Had another and didn't love her.
Peter learned to read and spell
And then he loved her very well.

First published in *Mother Goose's Quarto: or Melodies Complete,* in Boston, Massachusetts, around 1825, this verse seems to be American, pumpkins being native to North America and not England. But the Opies show its connection to an older verse:

Eeper Weeper, chimney sweeper,
Had a wife but couldn't keep her.
Had another, didn't love her,
Up the chimney he did shove her.

Clearly it harks back to some dreadful story of wife murder. It appears to have been laundered and turned into advice for good behaviour.

I had a little husband
No bigger than my thumb;
I put him in a pint pot
And there I bade him drum.
I gave him some garters
To garter up his hose
And a little silk handkerchief
To wipe his pretty nose.

According to *The Collected Historical Works of Sir Francis Palgrave,* in his "Antiquities of Nursery Literature," Tom Thumb was originally a dwarf of Scandinavian extraction, or Thaumlin, "little thumb of the Northmen." He is said to have been at the court of King Arthur, where he committed "marvelous acts of manhood," one of which was to venture on to a wife many times his size. He was buried in Lincoln Cathedral, where visitors could see his little blue flagstone grave in the minster; that is, until during renovations to modernize the stone was lost. But perhaps it is all a legend! In the tenth century there was a Danish work on "Swain Tomling, a man no bigger than a thumb, who would be married to a woman three ells and three quarters long." What is an ell? An ell is eighteen inches.

I wonder if Tom Thumb is any relation to . . .

Little Tommy Tittlemouse
Lived in a little house.
He caught fishes
In other men's ditches.

Little Miss Muffet

Sat on a tuffet
Eating her curds and whey.
Along came a spider
Who sat down beside her
And frightened Miss Muffet away.

The word "tuffet", if it ever was a word, has disappeared, living on only in this rhyme. Samuel McChord Crothers, in his story *Miss Muffet's Christmas Party,* in 1902, imagined that it was just there to make a rhyme. "A tuffet is the kind of thing that Miss Muffet sat on." But anthropologist and Mother Goose student Garth Haslam writes online that he found the word in a book published in 1578, where it describes a plant called the Royall Satyrion, which we now call an orchid: "Ye floures grow in a spiky bushe or tuffet, at the top of the stalke of a light purple colour, and sweet savour . . ."

So Miss Muffet sat on top of a flower. I bet she squashed it.

ittle Tom Tucker

Sings for his supper.
What shall we give him?
White bread and butter.
How shall he cut it
Without a knife?
How will he be married
Without a wife?

Singing for your supper means providing a service in order to receive a something, usually food, in return. The Baring-Goulds' *Annotated Mother Goose* dates the saying to the wandering performers who visited English inns and taverns. Their songs live on in nursery rhyme literature. Tommy Tucker was slang for orphan. Orphans were often destitute and had to beg, and because they had nothing, it would be difficult for them to marry.

Little Jack Horner
Sat in the corner
Eating a Christmas pie.
He put in his thumb
And pulled out a plum
And said, "What a good boy am I!"

Any lad might be a Jack, as any lass was a Jill. But Jack Horner was steward to the Abbot of Glastonbury in the time of Henry VIII and his dissolution of the monasteries. Sent to the king with a pie in which the deeds to twelve manors were concealed, Jack Horner "stuck in his thumb" and pulled out the deed to the Manor of Mells. Shortly after, a man named Thomas Horner moved into said manor. Horners live there today. But they claim their ancestor bought the property and was not called Jack. Still, it seems a bit fishy. Jack Horner has come to represent taking what you can get at any opportunity, or "taking care of number one." He also perhaps originated the practice of "having a finger in every pie."

And by the way, special items *were* baked into pies—sending gifts by way of pie was a kind of special delivery. If twelve deeds to monasteries could be, why not twenty-four blackbirds?

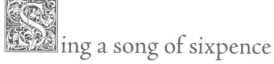

ing a song of sixpence
A pocket full of rye,
Four and twenty blackbirds
Baked in a pie.
When the pie was opened
The birds began to sing.
Wasn't that a dainty dish
To set before the king?

The king was in the counting-house
Counting out his money,
The queen was in the parlour
Eating bread and honey,
The maid was in the garden
Hanging out the clothes.
Along came a blackbird
And snipped off her nose.

Yes, you could bake birds in a pie. In Vita Sackville-West's lovely book *Nursery Rhymes,* she quotes a recipe from *The Italian Banquet* of 1589, "to make pies so that the birds may be alive in them and fly out when it is cut up."

ankee Doodle went to town

Riding on a pony,
He stuck a feather in his hat
And called it Macaroni!

We always sang this and marched around on my birthday on
the Fourth of July. I was a Yankee Doodle in my very Canadian
family. To me the rhyme was nonsense—until I discovered that
it dates from the Seven Years' War (1756–1763), when the
English and French battled in Quebec. The British were making
fun of the colonial soldiers whose wigs were not so stylish as
the "Macaroni," then all the rage.

Jack Spratt would eat no fat
His wife could eat no lean.
And so, betwixt them both, you see,
They licked the platter clean.

I always thought this was a little parable of marriage. Husband and wife prefer opposites, thereby balancing each other out. But no. The moral is: "Better to go to bed supperless than to rise in debt." So it isn't about alternating preferences to achieve harmony, but about "licking the platter clean"—thrift. The Opies call it a proverb and date it to 1639. Apparently, Jack Spratt was a common term for dwarf.

STORY RHYMES

These longer rhymes are examples of the "cumulative tale." Their
many verses amplify and alter the first, building to a climax. Common
in nursery rhymes thoughout the world, such tales are a delight to a
narrator who makes each verse different by changing her voice and
expression. Fairy tales as well are often cumulative, and feature malign
forces that grow stronger with each repetition—to be finally
overcome by a mere human.

     These rhymes are different from cumulative fairy tales, though.
They are not about the supernatural but about particular people in real
life. I see them as miniature novels. In fact, they may be novels in their
very earliest form. The chief interest of the novel, said Northrop Frye, is
"human character as it manifests itself in society."

This is the house that Jack built.

This is the malt that lay in the house that
Jack built.

This is the rat that ate the malt that lay in
the house that Jack built.

This is the cat that killed the rat that ate
the malt that lay in the house that
Jack built.

This is the dog that worried the cat that
killed the rat that ate the malt that
lay in the house that Jack built.

This is the cow with a crumpled horn
that tossed the dog that worried
the cat that killed the rat that ate
the malt that lay in the house that
Jack built.
This is the maiden all forlorn that milked
the cow with a crumpled horn that
tossed the dog that worried the
cat that killed the rat that ate the
malt that lay in the house that
Jack built.

This is the man all tattered and torn that
kissed the maiden all forlorn that
milked the cow with a crumpled
horn that tossed the dog that worried the cat that killed the rat that
ate the malt that lay in the house
that Jack built.

This is the priest all shaven and shorn that
married the man all tattered and
torn that kissed the maiden all
forlorn that milked the cow with a
crumpled horn that tossed the dog
that worried the cat that killed the
rat that ate the malt that lay in the
house that Jack built.

This is the cock that crowed in the morn that waked the priest all shaven and shorn that married the man all tattered and torn that kissed the maiden all forlorn that milked the cow with a crumpled horn that tossed the dog that worried the cat that killed the rat that ate the malt that lay in the house that Jack built.

Notice that this rhyme does not tell the story of Jack's house but of the people and things that touch it. The house is really an excuse. But it is something we can be shown. The real meaning of the verses is in the connectedness of cows and cats and maidens and marriages. Halliwell dates it to around 1550 on the evidence of "the priest all shaven and shorn." It was not published, however, until several hundred years later. These woodcuts are from an early version of this rhyme in the Osborne Collection, printed on its own as a child-sized book.

 ld Mother Hubbard
Went to the cupboard
To get her poor dog a bone.
When she got there
The cupboard was bare
And so the poor dog had none.

She went to the baker's
To buy him some bread.
When she came back
The dog was dead!

She went to the undertaker's
To buy him a coffin.
When she came back
The dog was laughing.

She took a clean dish
To get him some tripe.
When she came back
He was smoking his pipe.

She went to the alehouse
To get him some beer.
When she came back
The dog sat in a chair.

She went to the tavern
For white wine and red.
When she came back
The dog stood on his head.

She went to the fruiterer's
To buy him some fruit.
When she came back
He was playing the flute.

She went to the tailor's
To buy him a coat.
When she came back
He was riding a goat.

She went to the hatter's
To buy him a hat.
When she came back
He was feeding her cat.

She went to the barber's
To buy him a wig.
When she came back
He was dancing a jig.

She went to the cobbler's
To buy him some shoes.
When she came back
He was reading the news.

She went to the seamstress
To buy him some linen.
When she came back
The dog was spinning.

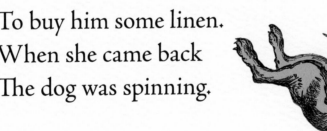

She went to the hosier's
To buy him some hose.
When she came back
He was dressed in his clothes.

The dame made a curtsy,
The dog made a bow.
The dame said, "Your servant."
The dog said, "Bow-wow."

This wonderful dog
Was Dame Hubbard's delight.
He could read, he could dance,
He could sing, he could write.
She gave him rich dainties
Whenever he fed
And erected this monument
When he was dead.

Few nursery rhymes portray true devotion. Interesting
that the object of that devotion is a dog. Apparently doting
on your dog is not a modern invention. Mother Hubbard
becomes the servant of her clever pet.

ho killed Cock Robin?
I, said the Sparrow,
With my bow and arrow
I killed Cock Robin.

Who saw him die?
I, said the Fly,
With my little eye
I saw him die.

Who caught his blood?
I, said the Fish,
With my little dish
I caught his blood.

Who'll make the shroud?
I, said the Beetle,
With my thread and needle
I'll make the shroud.

Who'll dig his grave?
I, said the Owl,
With my pick and shovel
I'll dig his grave.

Who'll be the parson?
I, said the Rook,
With my little book
I'll be the parson.

Who'll be the clerk?
I, said the Lark,
If it's not in the dark
I'll be the clerk.

Who'll carry the link?
I, said the Linnet,
I'll fetch it in a minute
I'll carry the link.

Who'll be chief mourner?
I, said the Dove,
I mourn for my love
I'll be chief mourner.

Who'll carry the coffin?
I, said the Kite,
If it's not through the night
I'll carry the coffin.

Who'll bear the pall?
We, said the Wren,
Both the cock and the hen
We'll bear the pall.

Who'll sing a psalm?
I, said the Thrush,
As she sat on a bush
I'll sing a psalm.

Who'll toll the bell?
I, said the Bull,
Because I can pull
I'll toll the bell.

All the birds of the air
Fell a-sighing and a-sobbing
When they heard the bell toll
For poor Cock Robin.

"Cock Robin" is another mini-novel presenting a cast of characters and their roles, this time in the rituals around death. Its particular magic is to solemnize the death of a bird, and to assign human mourning tasks to animals. The rhyme is very old, as evidenced by the rhyming of "owl" and "shovel." Like "The house that Jack built," it was often published in palm-sized booklet form and illustrated with woodcuts. In one version, the robin's murderer was sent to the gallows. Still, it was considered suitable for children. Ghoulish, but charming.

CHILDREN'S GAMES

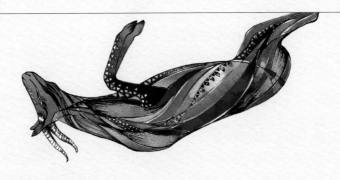

Ring around a rosie
A pocket full of posies
Hush-a! Hush-a!
We all fall down!

Mention nursery rhymes and their origins, and this one pops up. Everyone is sure he or she knows the history of this common game, in which children hold hands and dance in a circle. The "rosie" is a rash, a symptom of the Great Plague of London. "Posies" are the wild herbs that were carried as defence against the disease, and "hush-a" (in some versions it's "a-tishoo") is the sound of sneezing that victims made before the inevitable "fall down" pronounced them dead.

It all makes perfect sense. Except it's wrong. As the Opies tell us, this rhyme is not nearly old enough to reference the Great Plague, which took place in the seventeenth century. In fact, the rhyme didn't appear for the first time until the late nineteenth century, in Massachusetts, and did not include the phrase "Hush-a" (or "a-tishoo"). And in the game the fall was likely a graceful curtsy—and clearly not fatal, as the second verse shows:

> The cows are in the meadow
> Lying fast asleep
> A-tishoo! A-tishoo!
> We all get up again.

It's lovely to think that children curtsy and get up again instead of falling down dead. Even more pleasant is the old German belief, which perhaps *does* inform this rhyme, that certain children had the gift "to laugh roses."

The grand old Duke of York,

He had ten thousand men

He marched them up to the top of the hill

And he marched them down again.

And when they were up, they were up,

And when they were down, they

      were down,

And when they were only halfway up

They were neither up nor down.

The duke may have been Prince Frederick, Duke of York and Albany (1763-1827). His armies suffered heavy losses in Flanders in 1794, after which he was called back to England. Flanders, however, is very flat. So who knows? It seems to commemorate an indecisive military commander. But what is indecisive in a duke may be imaginative in a child.

    To me this was a birthday party game. We marched up and down, leaving out words 'though continuing the actions: "When they were up, they were ——"

On a mountain stands a lady,
Who she is I do not know.
All she wants is gold and silver,
All she gets is a big fat toe!

This is the perfect rhythm for double-dutch skipping. You jump out at "big fat toe!"

I'm a little teapot
Short and stout.
Here is my handle,
Here is my spout.
When I get all steamed up
Then I shout,
Tip me over
And pour me out.

Jack be nimble
Jack be quick
Jack jump over
The candlestick.

Jumping over candlesticks was a fortune-telling game. It was good luck if you made it over, and bad luck if you didn't, obviously.

London Bridge is falling down
Falling down, falling down.
London Bridge is falling down
My fair lady.

Build it up with wood and clay
Wood and clay, wood and clay.
Build it up with wood and clay
My fair lady.

Wood and clay will wash away
Wash away, wash away.
Wood and clay will wash away
My fair lady.

Build it up with bricks and mortar
Bricks and mortar, bricks and mortar.
Build it up with bricks and mortar
My fair lady.

Bricks and mortar will not stay
Will not stay, will not stay.
Bricks and mortar will not stay
My fair lady.

Build it up with iron and steel
Iron and steel, iron and steel.
Build it up with iron and steel
My fair lady.

Iron and steel will bend and bow
Bend and bow, bend and bow.
Iron and steel will bend and bow
My fair lady.

Build it up with silver and gold
Silver and gold, silver and gold.
Build it up with silver and gold
My fair lady.

Silver and gold will be stolen away
Stolen away, stolen away.
Silver and gold will be stolen away
My fair lady.

Set a man to watch all night
Watch all night, watch all night.
Set a man to watch all night
My fair lady.

Suppose the man should fall asleep
Fall asleep, fall asleep.
Suppose the man should fall asleep
My fair lady.

Give him a pipe to smoke all night
Smoke all night, smoke all night.
Give him a pipe to smoke all night
My fair lady.

This was originally a carol. "On Christmas Day in the morning" was the refrain. This was also a game we played at parties, with pairs of children holding their hands up to form a bridge and other children passing under.

BAD BEHAVIOUR

Tweedledum and Tweedledee
Agreed to have a battle
For Tweedledum said Tweedledee
Had spoiled his nice new rattle.
Just then flew down a monstrous crow
As black as a tar-barrel,
Which frightened both the heroes so
They quite forgot their quarrel.

There are almost too many famous names associated with
this rhyme, which is alleged to refer to the rivalry between
composers Handel and Bononcini, the one German-English
and the other Italian. The joke is that there was so little
difference between the two. The last two lines may have
been written by Jonathan Swift or Alexander Pope. Or not.

Ding dong, bell
Pussy's in the well.
Who put her in?
Little Johnny Flynn.
Who pulled her out?
Little Tommy Stout.
What a naughty boy was that
To try to drown poor pussy cat
Who ne'er did him any harm
But killed all the mice in the
farmer's barn.

"Will you walk into my parlour?" said
  the spider to the fly.
"'Tis the prettiest little parlour that
  ever you did spy
The way into my parlour is up a
  winding stair
And I've a many curious things to shew
  when you are there."

"Oh no, no," said the little fly, "to ask me
  is in vain
For who goes up your winding stair
Can ne'er come down again."

The Spider and the Fly is a poem by Mary Howitt, published in 1829. No child today would be fooled by such enticements.

Fee, fie, fo, fum,
I smell the blood of an Englishman.
Be he alive, or be he dead
I'll grind his bones to make my bread.

This curse appears in the story "Jack and the Beanstalk," and Shakespeare puts it in *King Lear*. The giant killer is a standard English hero. Sometimes he's just a tiny man, like Tom Thumb. Try to decode his curse: "Fum" might mean fume, "fee" means fie! "Fo" maybe means pooh! Altogether it becomes a blustering, sputtering rant. Here's another curse:

Tell-tale tit!
Your tongue shall be slit
And all the dogs in the town
Shall have a little bit.

Georgie Porgie, puddin' and pie
Kissed the girls and made them cry.
When the boys came out to play
Georgie Porgie ran away.

Georgie Porgie first appeared as Rowley Powley (for "roly poly"?) in the authoritative *Nursery Rhymes of England* by James Orchard Halliwell. Whoever he was, he seems to have been a bit of a coward. Some claims make the character George Villiers, the handsome and effeminate favourite of King James I.

I do not love thee, Doctor Fell,
The reason why I cannot tell
But this I know, and know full well:
I do not love thee, Doctor Fell.

The Opies say it's unclear if this rhyme originated with Tom Brown, a satirist of the seventeenth century admired by the likes of Jonathan Swift, and whether it referred to a notoriously strict dean of Christ Church college at Oxford. Earlier it was used by a gentleman to his wife:

> I love thee not, Nell
> But why I can't tell
> But this I can tell,
> I love thee not, Nell.

The Queen of Hearts
She made some tarts
All on a summer's day.
The Knave of Hearts
He stole the tarts
And took them clean away.
The King of Hearts
Call'd for the tarts
And beat the knave full sore.
The Knave of Hearts
Brought back the tarts
And vow'd he'd steal no more.

"That's a very moral one," says Mum. Agreed. This appears to be a little fable about bad behaviour and the efficacy of a good beating. "Knave" is a word that has gone out of use. He's a crafty fellow, a bit unprincipled. It also meant the jack in a pack of cards.

There was a little girl
Who had a little curl
Right in the middle of her forehead.
And when she was good
She was very, very good
But when she was bad, she was horrid!

Henry Wadsworth Longfellow, author of *The Song of Hiawatha,* in the mid-nineteenth century the most widely read American author, wrote this. I find his urging good behaviour on a girl annoying. Maybe he wrote it because the woman he loved rejected his proposals for seven years before she agreed to marry him. Many nursery rhymes by this time had become admonishments to children to behave well.

Three children sliding on the ice
Upon a summer's day.
As it fell out they all fell in,
The rest they ran away.

Now had these children been at home
Or sliding on dry ground,
Ten thousand pounds to one penny
They had not all been drown'd.

You parents all that children have
And you that have got none
If you would have them safe abroad
Pray keep them safe at home.

This too is an admonishment—but I like it because this time
it's the parents being called to task. "As it fell out" meant
"as it happened." A moral tale cheered up by the play with
oxymoron, or contradictory scenarios—ice on a summer day
and parents who have no children.

The Goops they lick their fingers
The Goops they lick their knives
They spill their broth on the tablecloth
Oh, they lead disgusting lives!
The Goops they talk while eating
And loud and fast they chew
And that is why I'm glad that I
Am not a Goop—are you?

The American author Gelett Burgess created the Goops in a series of popular books at the turn of the twentieth century. Intended to teach manners, they made rudeness quite a lot of fun. This is from *Goops and How to Be Them*.

PLAIN SILLINESS

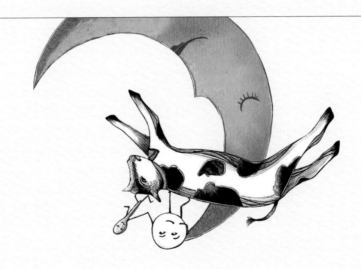

Mary, Mary, quite contrary
How does your garden grow?
With silver bells, and cockle shells
And pretty maids all in a row.

One of many theories identifies Mary as Mary, Queen of Scots, and her cockle shells as a punning reference to her husband Lord Darnley, who was, it was said, a cuckold. The joke depends on a homophone: two words that sound alike but have different spellings and meanings.

Alternately, Mary could be Bloody Mary, daughter of Henry VIII, and her "garden" may be her womb where she grew no heirs. The "pretty maids all in a row" could be a reference to her many miscarriages, and the "silver bells and cockle shells" could be colloquialisms for instruments of torture.

I think that's stretching it.

Three blind mice, three blind mice.
See how they run, see how they run.
They all ran after the farmer's wife
Who cut off their tails with a
        carving knife.
Did you ever see such a sight in your life
As three blind mice?

This rhyme existed in popular culture in the 1600s and only later was seconded to the nursery. It can be sung as a round. Violent and somehow disturbing, the rhyme is always illustrated by a vision of the farm woman running with her knife held high. But aren't the mice chasing her? There may be an allusion to Bloody Mary again, with the mice representing the three Protestant clerics she martyred—Latimer, Cranmer and Ridley. These little fellows and their prey are by Arthur Rackham, English illustrator of fairy tales and stories active in the early twentieth century, the 'Golden Age' of Illustrated books.

The man in the moon came down
     too soon
And asked his way to Norwich.
He went by the south and burnt
     his mouth
By supping on cold plum porridge.

Hey diddle diddle
The cat and the fiddle
The cow jumped over the moon.
The little dog laughed to see such sport
And the dish ran away with the spoon.

Sometimes a nonsense rhyme is just a nonsense rhyme.
It has been suggested that this one is a corruption of ancient
Greek, or is linked to Katherine of Aragon—who was known
as Katherine la Fidele (fiddle coming from *fidele,* or faithful)—
or constellations in the heavens: Taurus (the bull), Canis
Minor (the little dog) and the Big Dipper. Apparently none of
these explanations holds water. As the moral in my *Mother
Goose* reads, "It must have been a little dog that laughed, for
a great dog would be ashamed to laugh at such nonsense."

Rub-a-dub-dub
Three men in a tub
And how do you think they got there?
The butcher, the baker,
The candlestick-maker
They all jumped out of a rotten potato
'Twas enough to make a man stare.

An earlier version says "all of them gone to the fair . . . knaves
all three." The rub-a-dub bit is universally taken to suggest
that these rotters went to a sleazy fairground girlie show.

Clarence Milton's nose is funny
It turns up at the end.
His hair is red, his face is freckled,
But
 Clarence
   is
    my
     friend!

This is a "lost" Canadian nursery rhyme by Edith Lelean Groves, from *The Kingdom of Childhood* (1925), held in the Osborne Collection.

We are all in the dumps
For diamond are trumps
The kittens have gone to St. Paul's;
The babies are bit
The moon's in a fit
And the houses are built without walls.

———————— ❧ ————————

Nobody likes me, everybody hates me
Sitting in the garden eating worms,
        yum yum.
Long, thin, slimy ones; short, fat,
        fuzzy ones;
Oh, how they tickle when they squirm,
        yum yum.

TONGUE TWISTERS

eter Piper picked a peck of pickled
     peppers.
If Peter Piper picked a peck of pickled
     peppers,
How many pecks of pickled peppers did
     Peter Piper pick?

wan swam over the sea:
Swim, swan, swim!
Swan swam back again:
Well swum, swan!

WISDOM

Three wise men of Gotham
Went to sea in a bowl
And if the bowl had been stronger,
My song would have been longer.

"It is long enough." I love this moral, which appears in the
original printing. The story goes that the people of Gotham,
Nottinghamshire, pretended to be imbeciles so that the king
would not put a public highway through their town. They
undertook ridiculous tasks, like building a fence around a bird
in a bush, rolling a cheese downhill and presumably going
to sea in a bowl. The highway went elsewhere, but Gotham
became known as a town of fools.

A man of words and not of deeds
Is like a garden full of weeds
And when the weeds begin to grow
It's like a garden full of snow
And when the snow begins to fall
It's like a bird upon the wall
And when the bird away does fly
It's like an eagle in the sky
And when the sky begins to roar
It's like a lion at the door
And when the door begins to crack
It's like a stick across your back
And when your back begins to smart
It's like a penknife in your heart
And when your heart begins to bleed
You're dead, and dead, and dead, indeed.

This rhyme is in *Gammer Gurton's Garland*. It seems a bit long-winded, which is ironic.

arly to bed
And early to rise
Makes a man healthy,
Wealthy and wise.

---

 wise old owl sat in an oak
The more he heard, the less he spoke
The less he spoke, the more he heard
Why aren't we all like that wise old bird?

Birds of a feather flock together
And so will pigs and swine.
Rats and mice will have their choice
And so will I have mine.

Where 'ere you are this much I know,
Be careful of ITOLDUSO;
He loves to tease you when you're mad
Or makes you worse when you are sad.

❈

Now if one day upon the street
The wily RUMOUR you should meet,
Don't stop to speak, for if you do
You're sure to hear what is not true.

These two poems and others were written by Lieutenant Colonel Lionel Page, father of the poet P.K. Page. She believed they were composed while he was in the trenches fighting in the First World War. Her mother, Rose, illustrated them and bound them into a book, *Wisdom from Nonsense Land,* for her daughter.

For want of a nail the shoe was lost
For want of a shoe the horse was lost
For want of a horse the rider was lost
For want of a rider the message was lost
For want of a message the battle was lost
For want of a battle the kingdom was lost
And all for the want of a horseshoe nail.

The Opies tell us that this proverb can be traced back to
a sermon of 1629: "The loss of a nail, the loss of an army." It
became "the well-known catastrophe" and reportedly was
copied and hung on the wall of the Anglo-American Supply
Headquarters in London during the Second World War.

If wishes were horses,
Beggars would ride.
If turnips were bayonets,
I would wear one by my side.
And if ifs and ands
Were pots and pans,
There would be no work for tinkers!

This highly serviceable proverb appears to warn against extravagant hopes and at the same time stop children from quibbling with "ifs and ands." Its history dates to the 1500s.

BEDTIME

Muffle the wind;
Silence the clock;
Muzzle the mice;
Curb the small talk;
Cure the hinge-squeak;
Banish the thunder;
Let me sit silent,
Let me wonder.

This poem, entitled "Orders," is from *Complete Poems:
Part One* by A.M. Klein. Born one hundred years ago,
Klein preceded and influenced Leonard Cohen as a Jewish
Montreal poet. I like the message. There's perhaps more
need for it now than when he wrote it.

Little Joan Jump Up
Couldn't get her rump up
On the big bed
So she gave a little wiggle
And a cheating kind of squiggle
And slept on the carpet instead.

Some say this is a critique of the accessibility in the
guest cabins at the Jasper Park Lodge. Others connect it
with Jumping Joan: a mummer's song from the eighteenth
century celebrating a woman of poor reputation.

Here I am,
Little Jumping Joan.
When nobody's with me
I'm always alone.

As A was sitting half Asleep

"It's time for Bed," said B

C Crept into her little Cot

To Dreamland, off went D.

E closed his Eyes, F Fretful grew

"Good-night," G softly said

H Hurried up the wooden Hill

I put Itself to bed.

J Jumped for Joy when bedtime came

K Kissed good-night all round

L Lit the Lamp, M struck the Match

The land of Nod N found.

O Owned that he was Over-tired

To Pillowland P Pressed

Q Queried why it was so Quiet

When R Retired to Rest.
S went in Search of Slumberland
Too Tired was T To stay
U went Upstairs, V Vanished too
And W led the Way.
When X eXclaimed, "How Y does Yawn,"
With Zest responded Z,
"Dear me, it seems I'm last of all,"
And tumbled into bed.

Mystery and possible theft! This useful and little-known ditty combines the alphabet with a bedtime narrative. We know it appeared unsigned in print in the *Sunday Times* in Perth, West Australia, on May 6, 1934. Two months later it appeared as written by J. Wiltshire in the *Advertiser* in Victoria, Australia. I found it in *The Real Mother Goose* by J.B. MacDougall (1940).

ee Willie Winkie runs through
    the town
Upstairs and downstairs in his night-gown
Tapping at the window, crying at the lock
Are the children in their bed, for it's past
    ten o'clock?

Hey, Willie Winkie, are you coming in?
The cat is singing purring sounds to the
    sleeping hen
The dog's spread out on the floor, and
    doesn't give a cheep
But here's a wakeful little boy who will not
    fall asleep!

Anything but sleep, you rogue! Glowering
    like the moon
Rattling in an iron jug with an iron spoon
Rumbling, tumbling round about, crowing
    like a cock
Shrieking like I don't know what, waking
    sleeping folk.

Hey, Willie Winkie, the child's in a creel!
Wriggling from everyone's knee like an eel
Tugging at the cat's ear, and confusing all
    her thrums
Hey, Willie Winkie, see, there he comes.

Wee Willie Winkie, threatener of small children, came to life in a Scottish nursery rhyme written by William Millerand first published in 1841. In the original Scots it ran, "Wee Willie Winkie runs through the toon, upstairs an' doonstairs in his nicht-goon." In the same year, Hans Christian Andersen published his tale about the Sandman, another character said to command sleep from youngsters.

In winter I get up at night
And dress by yellow candle-light.
In summer quite the other way,
I have to go to bed by day.

I have to go to bed and see
The birds still hopping on the tree,
Or hear the grownup people's feet
Still going past me in the street.

And does it not seem hard to you,
When all the sky is clear and blue
And I should like so much to play,
To have to go to bed by day?

I related to this because in Edmonton the skies were
light until eleven at night in summer. By six in the morning I
could be found across the street helping Mrs. Gainer wash
her car. I loved this poem from my copy of *A Child's Garden of
Verses* by Robert Louis Stevenson, which Mrs. Gainer signed
to "my little helper."

Hush-a-bye, baby, on the tree top
When the wind blows the cradle will rock
When the bough breaks the cradle will fall
Down will come baby, cradle and all.

This has been called the first poem produced on North American soil. Then too it's an example of an early use of wind power. It is attributed to a Pilgrim boy who went to America on the *Mayflower* and observed the Natives hanging their birchbark cradles in the branches of trees. Of course once they got hold of this, the British were there to assign a moral: "This may serve as a warning to the proud and ambitious who climb so high that they generally fall at last."

Winken, Blinken and Nod one night
Sailed off in a wooden shoe
Sailed off on a river of crystal light
Into a sea of dew.
"Where are you going, and what do
        you wish?"
The old moon asked the three.
"We have come to fish for the herring fish
That live in the beautiful sea
Nets of silver and gold have we!"
Said Winken,
Blinken
And Nod.

The old moon laughed and sang a song
As they rocked in the wooden shoe
And the wind that sped them all
      night long
Ruffled the waves of dew.
The little stars were the herring fish
That lived in the beautiful sea.
"Now cast your nets wherever you wish
Never afeard are we"
So cried the stars to the fisherman three:
Winken,
Blinken
And Nod.

All night long their nets they threw
To the stars in the twinkling foam,
Then down from the skies came the
      wooden shoe
Bringing the fishermen home.
'Twas all so pretty a sail it seemed
As if it could not be
And some folks thought 'twas a dream
      they'd dreamed
Of sailing that beautiful sea.
But I shall name you the fishermen three:
Winken,
Blinken
And Nod.

Winken and Blinken are two little eyes
And Nod is a little head
And the wooden shoe that sailed the skies
Is the wee one's trundle-bed.
So shut your eyes while Mother sings
Of wonderful sights that be
And you shall see the beautiful things
As you rock in the misty sea,
Where the old shoe rocked the
      fishermen three:
Winken,
Blinken
And Nod.

If you took all the shoes out of nursery rhymes, what would
be left? This poem was written by the American journalist
Eugene Field, who died at age forty-five, leaving eight children.
His works were often illustrated by Maxfield Parrish. Field was
raised in Amherst, Massachusetts, the hometown of poets
Robert Frost and Emily Dickinson.

There is no Frigate like a Book
To take us Lands away,
Nor any Coursers like a Page
Of prancing Poetry—
This Traverse may the poorest take
Without oppress of Toll—
How frugal is the Chariot
That bears a Human soul.

Emily Dickinson was a reclusive, unmarried poet who dressed
exclusively in white, had a Newfoundland dog named Carlo and
wrote thousands of poems, most of which were unpublished
at the time of her death in 1886. Now she is recognized as one
of the major American poets.

From breakfast on through all the day
At home among my friends I stay,
But every night I go abroad
Afar into the land of Nod.

All by myself I have to go,
With none to tell me what to do—
All alone beside the streams
And up the mountain-sides of dreams.

The strangest things are there for me,
Both things to eat and things to see,
And many frightening sights abroad
Till morning in the land of Nod.

Try as I like to find the way,
I never can get back by day,
Nor can remember plain and clear
The curious music that I hear.

Robert Louis Stevenson was born in gloomy Scotland and as a child spent a lot of time sick in bed. Maybe it was a search for sun that led him to move to Samoa, where he died at forty-four while opening a bottle of wine. He remains one of the most translated authors in the world.

Matthew, Mark, Luke and John,
Bless the bed that I lie on.
Four corners to my bed,
Four angels round my head;
One to watch and one to pray
And two to bear my soul away.

"White Paternoster," as this rhyme is called, is a night spell
or incantation. Pagan witches used a corruption called "Black
Paternoster." It dates back to Celtic times in the English
countryside.

Star light, star bright,
First star I've seen tonight,
I wish I may, I wish I might
Have the wish I wish tonight.

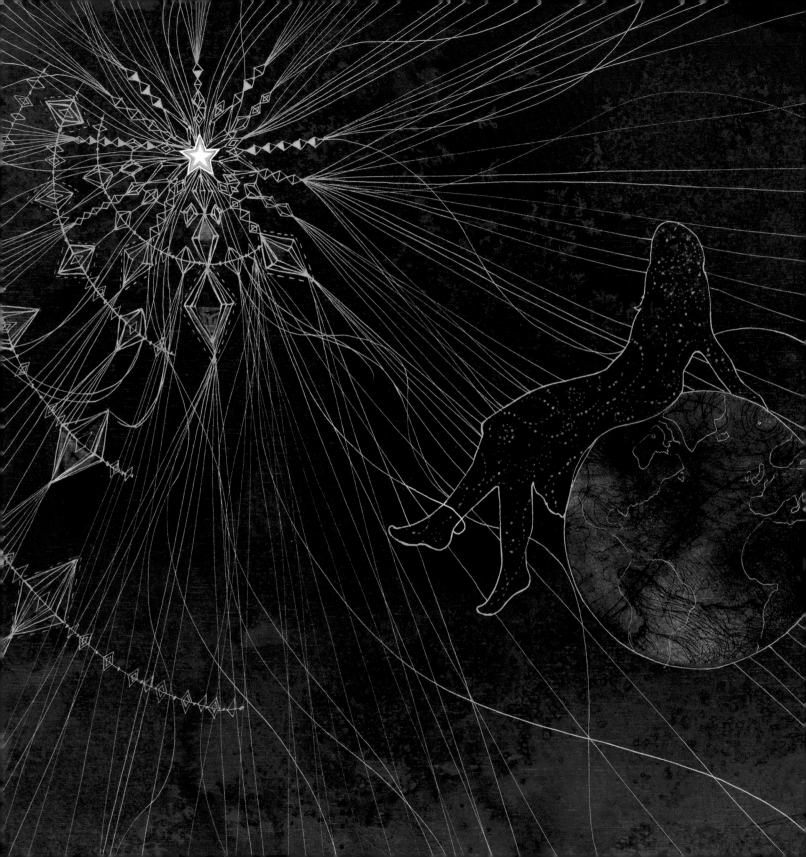

Twinkle, twinkle, little star
How I wonder what you are.
Up above the earth so high,
Like a diamond in the sky
Twinkle twinkle, little star
How I wonder what you are.

This poem was written by sisters Jane and Ann Taylor and published in 1806. Ann married; Jane didn't, becoming one of the first to write especially for children. "The Star" has been widely parodied; for instance, in this version recited by the Mad Hatter during the mad tea party in Lewis Carroll's *Alice's Adventures in Wonderland* (1865):

> Twinkle twinkle, little bat!
> How I wonder what you're at!
> Up above the world you fly,
> Like a tea-tray in the sky.

"The Bat" is said to refer to a mathematics professor at Oxford whose lectures went over his students' heads.

ight Thanks

Lightfall to
Nightfall, the
Earth settles
Deep,
Hunkering
Down in a
Blanket of
Sleep.

Careload by
Heartload, the
World falls
Away.
Tomorrow's
Tomorrow:
Be glad for
Today.

Dennis Lee is Canada's most loved children's poet. I can still recite half of his *Alligator Pie*: I read it hundreds of times to my kids. "Can you canoe in Kalamazoo? Can you canoe in Kamloops?" *Night Thanks* is Dennis in a more serious mood.

SOURCES

FOR REFERENCE

Baring-Gould, Cecil and William. *The Annotated Mother Goose*. New York: New American Library, 1962.

Bettleheim, Bruno. *The Uses of Enchantment*. New York: Vintage, 1975.

Haslam, Garth. "Mother Goose Mysteries: What Exactly Is a 'Tuffet'?" *Yahoo! Voices*. Last modified May 3, 2012.

MacDougall, J.B. *The Real Mother Goose: The Reality behind the Rhyme*. Toronto: Ryerson Press, 1940.

Opie, Peter and Iona, eds. *The Oxford Dictionary of Nursery Rhymes*. Oxford: Oxford University Press, 1988.

Palgrave, Sir Francis. "Antiquities of Nursery Literature," in *The Collected Historical Works of Sir Francis Palgrave*. Vol. 10. Edited by R.H. Inglis Palgrave. Cambridge: Cambridge University Press, 1922.

Sackville-West, Vita. *Nursery Rhymes*. London: Dropmore Press, 1947. (p. 32)

FOR RHYMES

Boyle, David. *Uncle Jim's Canadian Nursery Rhymes for Home and Kindergarten*. Illustrated by Charles William Jefferys. Toronto: Musson Book Co., 1908.

Burgess, Gelett. *Goops and How to Be Them: A Manual of Manners for Polite Infants*. New York: Frederick A. Stokes, 1900.

The Death and Burial of Cock Robin. London: Bishop, n.d., ca. 1840.

Dickinson, Emily. *The Poems of Emily Dickinson: Variorum Edition*. Cambridge, MA: The Belknap Press of Harvard University Press, 1998.

Ewing, Juliana Horatia. *The Brownies and Other Tales*. London: Bell & Daldy, 1870.

Friesen, Victor Carl. *The Windmill Turning: Nursery Rhymes, Maxims, and Other Expressions of Western Canadian Mennonites*. Edmonton, AB: University of Alberta, 1988.

Gordon, Robert Kay. *A Canadian Child's ABC*. Illustrated by Thoreau MacDonald. Toronto: Dent, 1931.

Groves, Edith Lelean. *The Kingdom of Childhood*. Toronto: Warwick Bros. & Rutter, 1925.

Halliwell, James Orchard. *The Nursery Rhymes of England*. London: Frederick Warne, 1886.

The House that Jack Built. London: Darton & Clark, n.d., between 1837 and 1845.

Klein, A.M. *Complete Poems: Part One*. Edited by Zailig Pollock. Toronto: University of Toronto Press, 1990.

Lee, Dennis. *So Cool*. Toronto: Key Porter, 2004.

Mother Goose's Nursery Rhymes. Chicago: M.A. Donohue, n.d., ca. 1900.

Mother Goose's Nursery Rhymes. New York: McLoughlin Brothers, n.d., ca. 1906.

Page, Rose and Lionel. *Wisdom from Nonsense Land*. Victoria, BC: Porcepic Books, 1991.

Rimbault, Edward F. *Nursery Rhymes, with the Tunes to which They Are Still Sung in the Nurseries of England*. London: Cramer, Beale & Co., 1846.

Ritson, Joseph. *Gammer Gurton's Garland*. London: R. Triphook, 1810.

Smith, Jessie Willcox. *The Jessie Willcox Smith Mother Goose: A Careful and Full Selection of the Rhymes*. New York: Dodd, Mead & Co. 1914.

Stacey, Robert. "*Under Some Malignant Star*": *The Strange Adventures of "Uncle Jim's Canadian Nursery Rhymes" by David Boyle and C.W. Jefferys, A lecture given at the Osborne Collection of Early Children's Books 14 November 1991*. Toronto: Toronto Public Library, 1992.

Stevenson, Robert Louis. *A Child's Garden of Verses*. New York: Henry Z. Walck, 1957.

The Tragical Death of an Apple Pie. London: Bishop, n.d., ca. 1840.

Young Canada's Nursery Rhymes. Illustrated by Constance Haslewood. London: Frederick Warne, n.d., ca. 1888.

INDEX OF FIRST LINES

Rhymes that are well known for their final lines are also indexed by final lines.
The names of authors, when known, are given in parentheses.